THIS BOOK BELONGS TO:

This book is dedicated to my husband Juan,

my father Miguel,

my mother Maria,

and my siblings Marcela, Miguel, Ana, and Luis.

Special thanks to Sharon Jacobson and

all the life teachers I have had.

Out Loud: June's Venture

Written by Luz Agudelo

Illustrated by Andres Restrepo

Layout by Jason Agudelo

Edited by Geddy Friedman & Michael Hernandez

Book Cover Design by Ana Maria Agudelo Berrio

ISBN 978-0-9983011-9-8

TABLE OF CONTENTS

ONE HOT SUNNY AFTERNOON

On a hot afternoon,
at the beach by the dune,
the wind crooned out this tune
about a girl named June.

Not so far from the strand,
where the sea meets the land,
June sat alone—like a lonely seabird on an isle.
Shyly, she tried to make friends with a smile,
glancing around with her eyes free of guile.

Nearby, her peers teamed up in groups of two or more,
for a school art competition
to sculpt a unique sand castle on the shore.
But June got left out, and it was hard to ignore.
Yet she still made the decision
to join by herself, though her heart felt sore.

1

In this contest, there was only one condition:
the kids had to build with sand—as was the tradition—
and scavenged stuff found within their reach,
along this peach-colored beach.

Crouching by her bucket, June tried to understand
how she could fit in, while
she and her peers began to style
tall towers by hand,
out of piles of wet sand.

Suddenly came Bill full of bluff,
a smug kid who presented a front of being tough.
Yet he avoided his sly downer feelings
by dumping them on other human beings.
Making his peers think they aren't good enough,
while he strutted around like he's hot stuff.

HATERS GONNA HATE

UGLY

Then Bill walked up to June and smiled smugly.
Pointing his finger he said with despise,
"Your castle looks weird and ugly."
Though it was trash-talk to put down and criticize,
June began to swallow the yuck of his taunting lies.

MY BAD

Later, Bill caught June off-guard
when he stomped on her sand castle hard,
leaving it smashed right before her eyes.
Next, Bill shrugged in disregard
and said, "My bad," while he sniggered faking surprise.

Shocked and upset, June whimpered in pain.
Yet the kids and grown-ups making up the crowd
didn't let June explain or speak out loud.
"Ignore him," the crowd said with disdain,
"Girl, toughen up, and don't complain.
Just build your sand castle again."

Although June exclaimed, "No fair,"
since the cold crowd standing there,
seemed unmoved as if they didn't care,
she thought it was her fault and fell into despair.

"Nobody likes you," said Bill to June with an evil stare,
messing with her mind with each pair,
of nasty words he spewed into the air.
Then, he threw rubbish at her hair,
giving June a big scare.

Like a dark cloud looming over her head,
June remembered with dread
the bashing words that Bill said.
Unsure about herself, she believed her accuser,
after all, she thought, *I do feel like a loser*.

Once her mind filled with negative gunk and stuff
about not being good enough,
June felt bad about who she was—kind of lame.
Teary, she hung her head in shame,
thinking herself worthless—like a piece of junk,
she fell into a "poor me" funk.

It was a clear sunny day,
but to June all around turned gloomy and gray.
Tormented by her mental chatter of self-doubt,
she ran off ready to drop out.

A caring kid named Jonas saw what occurred,
and he thought it was absurd.
He knew what Bill did was bullying and wrong.
Therefore, he refused to play along.

So, after June fled to hide from the crowd's nosy sight,
Jonas followed her to a rocky shore site,
where he caught up to her and said, "Hi,"
to let her know he was her ally.

DREAMING OUT LOUD

Quietly, the kids sat down on the gritty ground,

and listened to the ocean waves crashing around.

Relaxed and away from the crowds,

they breathed in and out with a soft sigh sound,

while gazing at the spun-cotton clouds

shifting shapes from oval to round.

Out of the blue, a bright castle-shaped cloud

flew by shining across the vast sky.

Like a beacon of light,

its gleam broke through June's foggy sight.

As her view cleared, she looked at things with a new eye.

Cracking a smile, she felt allowed to dream out loud.

Then, jolted by the sound of a bird's distress call,
Jonas and June sprang up with a yelp.
Quickly, they headed towards this shrieking bawl,
pretty sure it was a cry for help.

As the kids followed the shriek they heard,
in search for the troubled bird,
June called out, "Is everything okay?"
Soon, a voice came from not far away,
"Over here," it seemed to say.
Looking about they began to stray
from their current pathway,
stepping into the unknown with dismay.

With the scorching sun glaring down,

the kids searched all around.

Yet they only found here and there,

garbage and litter everywhere.

At that point they stopped and read

a worn-out sign that said, **"TRASH-MONSTER. BEWARE!"**

MONSTER ON THE BEACH

Then, like buzzing bees in a hive,
this pile of litter came alive.
Truck tires, bags, cans, bottles and a foam plate,
assembled into a monstrous shape.

With an evil grin and the face of a skull,
the trash-monster set out to break the gull's will,
by wrapping its clanky tail made of rusty tins,
around the bird's knees and shins.

As the kids stared with their mouths agape,
the Skull creature wouldn't let the gull escape.
So they knew this trash giant was no hero in a cape.

"Let me go!" cried Gull,

with pale cheeks and a gulp.

"Hey, you can't run from Skull,"

said the monster, while giving Gull an earful.

Despite the worry of this sad sight,

the kids did what was right,

by saying to Skull while being respectable,

"Bullying is unacceptable!"

Angered by the kids' honest feedback,
the monster charged, ready to attack,
screaming loudly, "I'll give you a smack!"
forcing Jonas and June to fallback.

Roaring forward with clenched toothy jaws,
Skull tried to catch the kids with its front paws,
made of broken glass, tins and razor-sharp claws,
for in this foul war, it would not pause.

TRASH-MONSTER
BEWARE!

THE PULL BACK

Rapidly and without delay,

Jonas and June ran away.

They knew they could no longer stay,

or they would become Skull's next prey.

"MWAA HAA-HAA! Go away, fools!"

mockingly shouted Skull.

Then, acting immature and cruel,

Skull used its rusty tin tail to shove Gull.

Menacing as if it wore a shiny gold crown,

wreaking havoc like a villain in a town,

Skull pushed Gull to the ground,

telling the bird, "You are easy to take down,"

while it laughed at Gull as if it were a clown.

But Gull didn't respond to all this with a frown.

Instead, it yelled, "HELP!" all around,

calling for a friend in this epic showdown.

FACING DARK FEARS

Once again the two kids heard Gull's call,
but this time they forgot they felt small.
So they didn't hesitate
to come back and set all things straight,
by saying to Skull, "Stop all this hate!"

"Bullying isn't cool, not at all,"
exclaimed a bothered June standing tall,
with hands on hips and legs apart,
truthfully from her heart.

"Just stop being a pest!"
shouted Skull annoyed and unimpressed.
"We're not!" Jonas countered in protest,
with his head up and a puffed-out chest.

Although Gull had beads of sweat on each feather,
trembling knees and a knot in its gut, it was still clever.
So, for the first time ever,
Gull heard the voice in its heart that said, "Whatever!
It's time to get away, better now than never."

BACK OFF

While Gull looked Skull in the eye, ready to conquer
its fear of this monster,
it let its own voice grow stronger,
and said, "BACK OFF! I'm not listening to you any longer."
Then, flapping its wings together,
Gull wrestled free from Skull's tight tether.

After Gull broke away,
it sensed how its inner power arose to stay,
making it feel brave, not a victim or Skull's prey.
Right there, Gull felt compelled to say,
"Thank you kids for showing me the way,
to speak up for myself without delay."

"Join us," said June, acting wiser and older,
as she put one hand around Gull's shoulder.
Frozen with surprise, Skull's face turned colder,
when it saw Gull becoming bolder.
Pointing at Skull, Jonas said, "Stop behaving like an ogre,
bullying time is over!"

BULLYING IS OVER

WHO'S LAUGHING NOW?

With its eyes wide in shock,
Skull couldn't even mock.
Once Skull saw Gull break free from its lock,
its pride was no longer tough as a rock.

Filled with remorse, Skull thought for a while,
hunched over, choosing not to be in denial,
owning its mean deeds and putting itself on trial,
gazing down it said, "I know I acted hostile,
by doing what is vile."

"See, I wasn't always this trash-creature.
I was once brand-new and good in nature.
But, after being used and abused,
I was thrown away like junk,
that couldn't be reused,"
said Skull with a metal clunk.
"Once a lot of trash piled upon me and grew,
I became a monster through and through.

"Now, I toss my emotional garbage right back at you,
and turn you into my trash bin on cue.
For when I dump on others my shame and spite,
by being impolite, I get thrust into the spotlight.
Like a celebrity, I can call the shots, too!
But what else can I do?
I don't have any clue."

LEARNING A LESSON

After Skull vented itself clean,
Gull said to the mosnter at this changing scene,
"I understand, but knocking my self-esteem,
like a tyrant, that's mean!
It didn't make you a king or a queen,
nor a bright star on the screen."

SNAP
OUT
OF IT

Next, Jonas also had to chime in,
with advice for Skull to take in,
"Don't use your burdens as an excuse,
to hurt others and continue with the abuse.
Instead, show a bit of grit to quit,
the cycle of bullying and snap out of it."

DARE
TO CARE

Right there, June happened to also share,
"Skull, now that you're self-aware,
be respectful and don't cause more despair.
You can do the right thing and dare
to switch fear for love and care.
Heal all your hurts and learn to play fair."

With no hard feelings Gull carried on,
and said, "Skull, we might get along,
but first, right your past wrongs.
Even though it's been long,
let the real Skull out to truly belong.
Make your heart beat like a drum—gentle yet strong,
by bringing about good deeds and songs."

In good faith Skull said, clear and true,
"I'm so sorry for the hurt I caused to all of you.
I hope it's not too late,
to let go of my woes and hate.
So I can begin to create,
a sweet life which is great."

A FLICKER OF LIGHT

Just before the sun set into the night,
Skull, the kids and Gull lit a campfire
and sat huddled around it for warmth and light.
Together, they all looked at the bright,
gingery-red flames with the desire,
to let go of the hurt and fright,
they piled up inside so tight,
seeking to be at peace and alright.

After each of them released their inner strife,
and tuned into their good feelings within,
finally happy in their own skin,
they stood up ready to embrace life.

"I know that I'm enough," said June to her crew,
as her sense of self and self-worth grew.
"So, it's okay to be me and it's okay to be you!"
Then, Jonas, Skull and Gull replied, "We think so, too."
Once again, they all felt brand-new.

Round dancing until the golden sun rose,
the kids, Skull and Gull chose,
to sing all night long, on key,
about living with glee:

"It feels good to be me,
on land or on the open sea.
I'm smiling, can't you see?
Steering my own ship, I'm finally free."

As Skull chanted this jolly note,
its heartfelt voice came up through its throat,
while it wished out loud to sail along seas remote,
like a castle-shaped boat.

On the spot, Skull used its inner gift,
to allow its body to shape-shift.
With its tires, cans and bottles shuffling around,
making a jangly clunk sound,
the trash-monster turned into a castle-like ship, so swift,
that it reached the shoreline with a quick drift.

FAR SEAS ADVENTURE

Once Gull, Jonas and June
saw Skull, so attuned
with its better self, oh so soon,
these three just nearly swooned.

In a friendly gesture,
the children and Gull, with great pleasure,
embarked with Skull on an unknown far-seas venture,
open to discover a new adventure.

Confidently, they rode the waves feeling pleased,
breathing in the salty breeze,
surfing along the berry blue seas,
gliding away with ease.

After what seemed like a long while,
a whistle's blow came from a mile.
Yet the kids still heard the piercing sound,
calling all contestants to gather round
and show the castles they built up from the ground.

With no time left to sper
Jonas, June and Gull sailed back to atten
this contest with their trash-castle frien
Together, they left behind the seas with no er
where dreams and daytime bler

TWEEEE

THE COMEBACK

Once they reached the far shore,
feeling so proud of themselves like never before,
Gull spread its wings to soar.

Rising through the sky, it flew,
circling around right over its crew.
Then, Gull waved goodbye because it knew,
it was time to go on and start anew.
While its friends waved back, Gull blurred out of view.

Next, the kids pushed Skull out of the water onto land,
this unique castle-boat made of sand,
truck tires, bottles, cans and something more:
the gift of **SELF-WORTH** at its core.

Although some school peers, looking in awe,
said they liked the trash-castle boat a lot,
Bill opened his mouth, only to point out a flaw.
Yelling, he taunted, "June, is that all you got?
Then your sandcastle isn't worth squat!"

Soaking up the warmth of the sun,

with her bare feet planted in the ground,

breathing slowly counting one by one,

June didn't run, wait for rescue or cry.

No more self-pity or feeling shy.

To the bully's put-downs, she refused to comply.

Asking Bill with a cool voice and a firm stare,

June said, "Well, what do you know? Why do you care?"

Trying to give June doubts and fear,

Bill argued with a snide sneer,

"I know your castle looks creepy and lame."

But June didn't take in the bully's shame,

no longer falling for his twisted mind game.

To Bill's taunts and lies June said, "Nay,"
muting in her head all that he came to say.
Now she chose to thrive by,
becoming her own greatest ally.
So, putting things to rest,
June said, "I like my sandcastle best."
"I'm just telling it like it is," Bill replied in protest.

Shaking her head side to side, June disagreed.
Trusting her own point of view indeed,
she felt confident and proud,
to speak her heart out loud,
saying to Bill with a 'meh' attitude,
"Mind your own business dude!"

Once Bill saw June acting stronger,
noticing he couldn't poke at her emotions any longer,
he left saying, "This isn't funny anymore."
From then on, his bullying towards June was done for.

Pumping her fist and taking a bold stand,
June drew a mental line in the sand,
that said, "My mind is safe and sound.
Bullies, don't come around."

KEEP ON KEEPING ON

After June took the risk of facing these fearsome guys
and managed to prevail,
the **COURAGE** she found was the best prize
to take with her across her life's trail.

With nothing to prove and no one to impress,
June dusted herself off with finesse.
Now, deep down, she felt like a priceless jewel,
so she stopped seeking others' approval.

Once again, sitting crouched side by side,

having their feet tickled by the foaming tide,

feeling good about what they had built and done,

Jonas, June and Skull continued with their fun.

With a playful twinkle in their eyes, they smiled,

letting their imagination run wild,

mixing and stacking more damp sand,

into this unique trash-castle boat, hand in hand.

Kneading this brown dough with each finger,

the kids and Skull allowed their wonder to linger.

While the breeze blew upon her face,
June tilted her head up with grace,
no longer worried about things,
such as winning the contest's first place.
Welcoming the air's soft embrace,
like a bird carelessly flapping its wings,
she gently swayed to the wind's croon,
humming along with its whispered tune.

Determined to be who she is every day,
June let out a sudden, "Yaaayyy"
cheering herself all the way.
Calmly steering through life's crowd,
feeling lighter than a summer cloud,
she felt ready to live **OUT LOUD**.

Made in the USA
Columbia, SC
10 February 2020